Hello, Stars!

A Sleepytime Tale
of God's Loving Presence

By Sheila Walsh ★ Art by Deborah Maze

A CHILDREN OF FAITH BOOK *published by* WATERBROOK PRESS

HELLO, STARS!
PUBLISHED BY WATERBROOK PRESS
2375 Telstar Drive, Suite 160
Colorado Springs, Colorado 80920
A division of Random House, Inc.

ISBN 1-57856-336-4

Published in association with the literary agency of Alive Communications, Inc.,
7680 Goddard Street, Suite 200, Colorado Springs, CO 80920.

Children of Faith, 436 Main Street, Suite 205, Franklin, TN 37064

Visit Children of Faith at http://children-of-faith.com

Printed in the United States of America
2001—First Edition

10 9 8 7 6 5 4 3 2 1

He merely spoke,

and the heavens were formed

and all the galaxies of stars.

PSALM 33:6

You look tired, little one.
Your eyes are sleepy too.
So let me tell a story
from the great land of Gnoo.

One starry night not long ago,
in a house that's painted white,
a mommy tucked her boy in bed
beneath the twinkling lights.

"I'll go to sleep now, Mommy dear,
but can you tell me please,
if God bends down to see my face,
why can't I see his knees?

"Why can't I hear him laugh and sing
or look at him and say,
'Hello there, God. This is my room.
I'd love if you could stay'?"

"Go to sleep now, darling lamb,"
Sam's mommy said that night.
"I know God heard your questions.
May the answers come with light."

That night Sam watched the brilliant stars,
which sparkled like the sea,
a million dancing fairy lights
as bright as bright can be.

Their silver glow lit up his room
and kissed his golden hair.
"I think God's like the stars," Sam whispered
to his sleepy bear.

When morning came, Sam rubbed his eyes
and tumbled out of bed.
"My bear is gone! Where can he be?"
"We'll find him," Mommy said.

The sky was full of clouds that night.
They blanketed the moon.
"Dear God, please help me find my bear.
It's dark here in my room.

"Oh, Mommy! Why's the sky so black?
The stars have gone away.
If God is like the stars above,
how will he hear me pray?"

The next night it was raining,
then the next night, on and on...

And Sam stopped looking for the stars.
He knew that they were gone.

But then one winter's evening
when he crept out of his bed,
Sam heard his mommy talk to God,
and this is what she said:

"Dear God, please show my darling child
that you are watching him."
Sam tiptoed past his mommy's door
and back into his room.

"Oh, Mommy, come! Come quickly now!"
Sam called. "You have to see!
The stars are shining bright as bright.
I think God's watching me!"

The night was cold and crystal clear
and lit up like a tree,
with silver stars that winked at Sam
as far as he could see.

He sat there in his rocking chair
and watched for quite a while.
"Hello, stars! Welcome to my room."
His mommy rocked and smiled.

"The stars have always been there, Sam,
as bright as bright can be.
But clouds and rain and winter storms
just made them hard to see.

"And God is always with you,
when you're happy, when you're sad.
When you do those very naughty things
and things that make him glad."

"So go to sleep now. Close your eyes
and say this little prayer,
'Hello, God! Welcome to my room.
I'm glad that you are here.'"

I hope you liked Sam's story
from the great land of Gnoo.
So close your eyes now.
Go to sleep.
God's watching over you.